Amy Owen
22 Gratley Croft
Huntington Cannock
Staff's

WS12 4PY

The
Snow Queen

Illustrated by
Rie Cramer

GEDDES & GROSSET

Once upon a time there was a bad wizard who had made a magic mirror. In it everything good looked ugly. The wizard showed it to the nasty little imps, his pupils, and they took the mirror everywhere. They even wanted to see how heaven would look in it. But as they flew higher and higher the mirror shook and shook till it slipped from their hands and broke into a million pieces, some as small as a speck of dust. If a tiny grain got in a child's eye, everything he saw looked bad, and if a piece got into his heart, that heart turned to ice! And now just listen.

boy named Kay and a little girl called Gerda lived in a big town in houses next to one another. They were very poor, but even so each had a garden in which grew a rambler rose. The roses twined around the windows and made a little bower, underneath which on summer days the children often sat together.

One day Kay suddenly cried:

"Ow, I've got something in my eye! Ow, my heart, now it is in my heart!"

He rubbed his eye and said, "It's gone." But it was a splinter of the magic mirror, so now poor Kay saw everything twisted, and his heart was frozen.

Little Kay was quite changed and now made fun of little Gerda and her grandmother. When winter came, snow lay thick on the square, and Kay took his toboggan to play with other children. One day a white sledge appeared, drawn by a white horse; in the sledge sat a figure in white furs. Kay tied his toboggan to it and away they sped, farther and farther, until they had passed through the town gate. Kay was badly scared. He tried to undo the knot, but he could not. When at last the sledge stopped, a beautiful lady stepped out, and Kay knew at once that she was the Snow Queen.

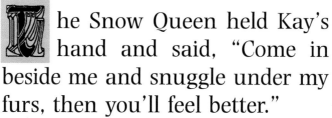he Snow Queen held Kay's hand and said, "Come in beside me and snuggle under my furs, then you'll feel better."

She kissed him lightly on the forehead, and her kiss was as cold as ice. Then she kissed him again and he forgot the cold, Gerda, and everyone else at home. He was not afraid any more, and told her how cleverly he could add and multiply and divide. She smiled and took him into her sledge and up they went in the air. Far beneath them wolves were howling and crows croaking. When night came he slept at the Snow Queen's feet while on and on they went to the far north.

RIE CRAMER

Oh, how bitterly little Gerda cried! People thought he had been drowned in the river. Then spring came and the roses budded again.

"Kay is dead and gone," said Gerda.

"Not so," said the sunshine.

"He is dead," she told the swallows.

"Don't believe it," they replied, and in the end Gerda did not think it was true. Then one day she said to the river:

"I will give you my new red shoes, if you will bring me to Kay."

Gerda got into a boat and threw her shoes in the water. The boat drifted away and took little Gerda with it.

he drifting boat came at last to a strange little house. It stood in a cherry orchard, and wonderful flowers grew in the garden. Two wooden soldiers stood guard beside it. An old woman came out, wearing a big hat painted with flowers. She pulled up the boat and lifted Gerda out of it. Gerda told her all about Kay, and the old woman took her into the house, where she ate as many cherries as she wanted, while the old woman combed her hair with a magic comb which made Gerda forget about Kay. The old woman wanted Gerda to stay with her; she always had wanted a little girl for her own.

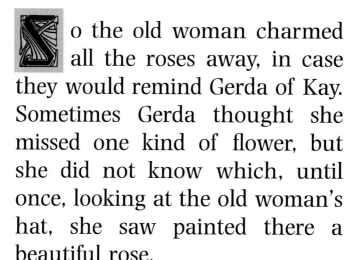

So the old woman charmed all the roses away, in case they would remind Gerda of Kay. Sometimes Gerda thought she missed one kind of flower, but she did not know which, until once, looking at the old woman's hat, she saw painted there a beautiful rose.

"Why are there no roses here?" Gerda asked, and then she remembered Kay and cried. Where her tears fell sprang up a rose tree; she kissed the flowers and asked about Kay.

"He is not dead," the roses said.

"Well, I must look for him," said Gerda. Then she opened the gate and went barefoot into the wide, wide world.

hen Gerda sat down to rest, a big crow came and asked what she was doing. Gerda told him, and asked if he had seen Kay. "Perhaps," said the crow, "but surely he has forgotten you for the Princess?"

"What Princess?" asked Gerda, and he told her about a Princess who had promised to marry the man clever enough to amuse her with stories. All had failed, till there came a boy with a toboggan, whose tales were wonderful. So she married him. "I know, for my wife is living in the palace."

"Oh, will you take me there?" cried Gerda. "I will," said the crow, "tonight."

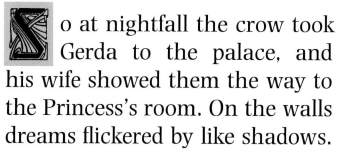So at nightfall the crow took Gerda to the palace, and his wife showed them the way to the Princess's room. On the walls dreams flickered by like shadows.

Gerda held her little lamp and looked at the Prince in his bed. She saw a brown neck and dark hair. Oh, it must be Kay! She called his name, then the Prince awoke and sat up—and it wasn't Kay at all!

She told her story to the Prince and Princess, and the Princess took her to sleep in her own bed.

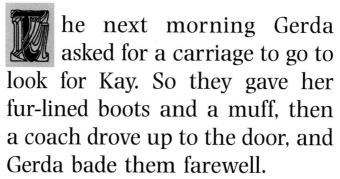

he next morning Gerda asked for a carriage to go to look for Kay. So they gave her fur-lined boots and a muff, then a coach drove up to the door, and Gerda bade them farewell.

On rolled the coach through a forest, until it was stopped by robbers who pulled little Gerda out. A robber woman drew out a big knife, but before she could hurt Gerda her own daughter jumped on her back and bit her ear.

"She must play with me!" the robber girl cried. "She must give me her boots and her muff and sleep in my bed."

So they all drove off to the robbers' castle.

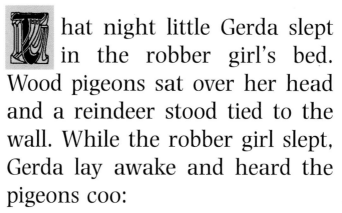

hat night little Gerda slept in the robber girl's bed. Wood pigeons sat over her head and a reindeer stood tied to the wall. While the robber girl slept, Gerda lay awake and heard the pigeons coo:

"We have seen Kay. He was sitting in the sledge of the Snow Queen."

"Where did they go?" cried Gerda.

"To Finland," the pigeons said.

Next morning Gerda told the robber girl everything the pigeons had said. She nodded and said:

"All right. I will turn the reindeer loose so that it can carry you to Finland. Do you know the way, reindeer?"

The reindeer jumped for joy, for it had been born there. The robber girl gave Gerda back her fur-lined boots, but she kept the muff. Gerda kissed the robber girl goodbye, and away sped the reindeer, across the marshes and mountains, running day and night. The food that the robber girl had given them was finished when at last they reached Finland. There they stopped at a small house and knocked at the door. A Finnish woman let them in, and they told her the story of Kay, Gerda first giving her her boots and her gloves, for the old woman was very poor.

After hearing Gerda's sad story the old Finnish woman replied, "The splinters must be removed, or the Snow Queen will keep him for ever." She then told the reindeer, "You must take Gerda to the bush of red berries, then come back to me."

The reindeer took Gerda to the bush with the red berries, then kissed her goodbye, the tears streaming from his eyes. So little Gerda stood alone in the icy cold of Finland. She said a prayer, and her breath froze into an army of little angels who chased away the ugly ice-monsters. Then Gerda went on.

Kay had forgotten all about little Gerda, and was enjoying staying in the castle of the Snow Queen. The Snow Queen sat on a throne in the middle of a frozen lake, while Kay played with ice blocks.

When little Gerda reached the palace, the Snow Queen was away, and Kay was sitting all alone in the great empty hall.

Gerda knew him at once, and kissed him and held him tight. "Kay!" she cried. "Kay, have I found you at last?" But he did not answer, nor did he know her, because his heart was frozen.

hen Gerda's tears fell on his chest, and sank down to his heart and melted it. He recognized Gerda and burst into tears, which washed the speck of the magic mirror from his eye.

"Gerda!" he cried, "at last!"

Gerda laughed and wept for joy. Hand in hand they went off. At the bush with the red berries, the reindeer stood waiting. On they went with him till they reached the house of the Finnish woman. There they took leave of the reindeer and went on their way until they came to their own town! Their roses were in bloom, and Kay and Gerda were home again at last.

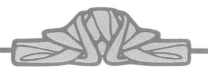

ISBN 1 85534 151 4

2 4 6 8 10 9 7 5 3 1

Printed in U.A.E.